DANGEROUS DINOSAURS

by
Adam Hibbert

Scaly Survivors
Dinosaurs roamed the planet for 160 million
years. Humans have a long way to go—we've
only been here for $1\frac{1}{2}$ million years!

TERRIBLE LIZARDS

Dinosaurs roamed the Earth for 160 million years before suddenly dying out about 65 million years ago— long before humans were around. From huge treetop-nibbling plant-eaters to chicken-sized hunter-killers, dinosaurs in all shapes and sizes reigned as the supreme land animals.

Tyrannosaurus rex scavenging

SUITS YOU, SIR!

Based on preserved skin impressions, we know that dinosaurs were scaly, but actual skin decays away, so we can only guess their colors!

DINO'S DOMAIN

Dinosaurs first appeared about 225 million years ago, when all the world's dry land was still one continent, called Pangaea. There were huge deserts inland where survival was difficult. But as Pangaea began to split into pieces, the climate became more favorable, and many parts of the world became a "dinosaur heaven"!

DINO DYNASTY

Paleontologists (scientists who study dinosaur remains) divide the age of the dinosaurs (also called the Mesozoic Era) into three main parts. The first dinosaurs appeared during the Triassic Period, from about 248 to 206 million years ago (mya). Some of the largest dinosaurs thrived during the Jurassic Period, from 206 to 142 mya. It was at the end of the Cretaceous Period (142 to 65 mya) that all dinosaurs disappeared.

BIG NEWS

It was only around 150 years ago that scientists realized a whole world of fantastic animals had existed before humans. This news promised a revolution in biology. In 1841, the scientist Richard Owen named the animals dinosaurs, meaning "terrible lizards." Dinosaurs are also known as archosaurs—"ruling reptiles."

NICE LEGS

Dinosaurs had specialized hips, knees, and ankles that allowed them to tuck their legs under their bodies. They were able to walk and run extremely efficiently.

GREAT-GRANDPA BRACHIOSAURUS

Even if you eat a lot of trees, it would take a very long time to get this big. *Brachiosaurus* may have lived to be 125!

BRAIN BONUS

Where were the first *Seismosaurus* fossils found?

a) Alaska
b) Florida
c) New Mexico

If you stood next to a *Brachiosaurus* leg, how high would you reach?

a) up to its shoulder
b) just past its knee
c) just below its hip

Sauropods did not use their long tails...

a) to pick their teeth
b) for balance
c) as a weapon

(answers on page 32)

EARTH QUAKER!

Sauropods may have been able to rear up on their hind legs to reach the treetops. One sauropod skeleton in the Museum of Natural History in New York City is shown rearing to a height of 56 feet (that's the height of three giraffes)! Bones of even bigger sauropods have been discovered. The biggest one of all was *Seismosaurus* (SIZE-moh-SORE-us). From nose to tip of tail, it was longer than three school buses and weighed as much as fifteen elephants!

TOP TIP

Small sauropods called ankylosaurs (an-KEE-loh-sores) were only 20 feet long, and they were rather slow. But they had thick armor on their backs, and predators probably had to try and tip them over to reach their soft bellies. It wouldn't have been easy!

GINORMOUSAURUS!

Ankylosaurus

A family of truly tremendous dinosaurs called sauropods (SORE-oh-pods) lived during the Jurassic Period. They were peaceful plant-eaters (herbivores) that probably traveled in herds, grazing on tough plants that may have taken days to digest. To support their enormous body weight, they had legs as thick as pillars.

HUGE HUNGER

As the biggest land animals to ever exist, sauropods must have eaten amazing amounts of plant food to stay alive. *Brachiosaurus* (brak-ee-oh-SORE-us), as tall as a four-story building, could have easily reached the tops of trees to nibble at the tastiest branches. Other dinosaurs, such as *Edmontosaurus* (ed-MON-toh-SORE-us), had hundreds of flat teeth that allowed them to grind up tough seeds and leaves that grew closer to the ground.

Brachiosaurus

SUPER SWIMMERS

Despite their enormous size, sauropods could move easily in the water. By studying fossilized footprints in what was once a lake in Texas, paleontologists have discovered that sauropods used their front feet to tiptoe along the bottom.

KING LIZARD

When paleontologists began to uncover a dinosaur skull
in Montana in 1902, they could hardly believe what they
were seeing. Emerging from the 70-million-year-old rock was
the toothy grin of one of the most fearsome meat-eaters
(carnivores) ever to have stalked the Earth—*Tyrannosaurus rex!*

KING OF THE KILLERS

Looming out of the jungle mists, *Tyrannosaurus* (tie-RAN-oh-SORE-us) *rex*
was 40 feet of muscle, claw, and tooth. Its mouth was lined with serrated-
edged teeth like 7-inch steak knives and could open wide enough to
swallow prey as large as
a 12-year-old human in
one gulp!

Tyrannosaurus rex skull and upper skeleton

NOT ENTIRELY ARMLESS!

The *T-rex* had such effective biting equipment that
it didn't use its forearms as weapons; they were
tiny and were probably only used to help it
stand up after a nap.

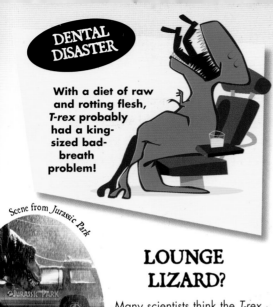

DENTAL DISASTER

With a diet of raw and rotting flesh, *T-rex* probably had a king-sized bad-breath problem!

Scene from *Jurassic Park*

BRAIN BONUS

During which part of the dinosaur age did *T-rex* rule the world?

a) at the very end
b) from beginning to end
c) only at the beginning

Which parts of *T-rex* are most commonly found?

a) hip bones
b) teeth
c) claws

How long was the *Tyrannosaurus's* "smile"?

a) 2 feet
b) 3 feet
c) 7 feet

(answers on page 32)

LOUNGE LIZARD?

Many scientists think the *T-rex* was too big and slow to run after its own prey. They suggest that it relied on scaring other predators away from a kill. Others think that it approached prey by stealth and then pounced.

BIGGER & BADDER

Some fossils suggest that *T-rex* may *not* have been the supreme meat-eater. Paleontologists have recently unearthed a predator named *Carcharodontosaurus* (kar-CARE-oh-DON-toh-SORE-us), meaning "shark-toothed reptile." At 50 feet in length—longer than a tanker truck—the fossilized skeleton of this tremendous creature is larger than any *T-rex* specimen ever found.

SMALL BUT DEADLY

The ferocious *Deinonychus* was 10 feet long from the tip of its nose to the end of its tail, but its head would reach only to a man's shoulder, and it weighed a mere 165 pounds. Like its smaller cousin, *Velociraptor* (vel-AW-si-rap-tor)—made famous but filmed oversize in *Jurassic Park*—*Deinonychus* must have made up for its small size with its lightning-quick responses.

BRAIN BONUS

How do we know which dinos ate meat?
a) They lived longer.
b) They were fatter.
c) by the shape of their teeth

Some dinos used their claws to help them...
a) fly
b) dig
c) swim

Where are dinosaur fossils not found?
a) on the moon
b) South America
c) Antarctica

(answers on page 32)

Megalosaurus tooth with sawlike edge

SAWTOOTH

Few meat-eaters had such amazing claws, but they made up for it by having terrible teeth! The teeth of *Megalosaurus* (MEG-ah-loh-SORE-us) were each nearly 8 inches long, with a sawlike edge for ripping through meat. Meat-eaters' teeth were constantly replaced so that they always had a full set of sharp chompers.

TOOTH AND CLAWS

Scientists once argued that dinosaurs must have been cold-blooded, sluggish, and probably a bit stupid. But in 1964, a terrifying new predator was unearthed in Montana that gave everyone a shock. It was the small, speedy, big-brained, and obviously vicious *Deinonychus* (die-NON-i-KUS), or "terrible claw."

Deinonychus

LICENSE TO KILL

Deinonychus was designed for pursuit, with a large but very light skull. Its "terrible claw" was a 5-inch switchblade in a sheath on each powerful rear foot. A kick from this deadly weapon could slice open the belly of large prey, causing it to collapse to the ground; *Deinonychus* could then go to work with its razor-sharp teeth.

SNAGGING LUNCH

Deinonychus had unusually well-developed arms and wrists, similar to humans in the number of ways they could move. For difficult prey, *Deinonychus* may have jumped into the air to snag a large plant-eater with its arms. It could then slash with its hind legs, using its stiff tail for balance.

KEEP 'EM KEEN

Along with its scary toenails, *Deinonychus* also had three sharp claws on each front foot.

HUNTING IN PACKS

Scientists have suggested that *Deinonychus* might have been a social hunter, roaming the prehistoric landscape in family packs, in much the same way as lions or wolves do today. This means that other small meat-eating dinosaurs might also have been active predators—not just scavengers.

Triceratops

RUN FOR IT!

Some of the smaller dinosaurs could run almost as fast as a racehorse—up to 35 miles per hour!

GO TEAM!

By working as a team, *Deinonychus* could have charged into herds of large, plant-eating dinosaurs, singling out the young and weak for an easy meal. But they were also capable of catching agile prey; their tails were specially made for flicking sideways, letting them whip around tight corners at high speed.

CRAFTY KILLERS

Hunting in packs takes brains! Dinosaurs that worked together would need to be able to communicate with each other (as wolves do today, for example) and might have set up sophisticated ambushes for their prey. If they were truly this crafty, they were as clever as any carnivore alive today.

WALL OF FEAR

If plant-eaters had to defend themselves from packs of meat-eaters, they might have responded as elephants do today. If so, the adults would have put themselves between their babies and the predator, forming a formidable barrier. Even the hungriest carnivore must have been afraid of a wall of *Triceratops* (try-SERR-a-tops), herbivores with fearsome horns.

SPEED DEMON

Velociraptor, the swift hunter, was discovered in Mongolia in 1924. But it was only after discovering its cousin, *Deinonychus*, that scientists realized such animals might have hunted in packs. *Velociraptor* could easily have run down and killed much bigger dinosaurs if it had worked in a group.

A *Velociraptor* in a scene from *The Lost World: Jurassic Park*

MURDEROUS MEAT-EATERS

Life for meat-eating dinosaurs could be tough—if they wanted dinner, first they had to hunt it down and kill it! But *Allosaurus* (al-oh-SORE-us) and its close relatives were the best hunters the world has ever known.

BRAIN BONUS

During what period did *Allosaurus* live and hunt?

a) Triassic (210 mya)
b) Jurassic (150 mya)
c) Cretaceous (70 mya)

Why did the 74 teeth of *Allosaurus* curve backward?

a) for easy cleaning
b) for a better grip on prey
c) for tearing up leaves

When was the first big meat-eating dinosaur described by a scientist?

a) 1824
b) 1845
c) 1902

(answers on page 32)

CREEPY CANNIBAL

If an unusual *Coelophysis* (SEEL-oh-FIH-sis) fossil from New Mexico is any indication, this early meat-eater was especially nasty. Just where its belly would have been, scientists have found the bones of several *Coelophysis* babies—so this dinosaur was a cannibal!

Allosaurus

EYE-SPYASAURUS

Allosaurus had fantastic eyesight. Its eyes were large, which would have helped it to hunt even in the low light of dawn or dusk.

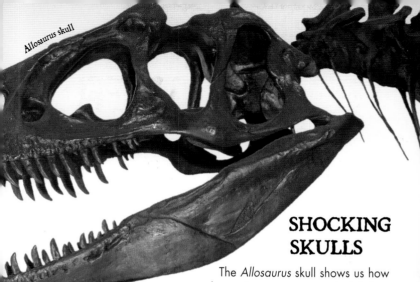

Allosaurus skull

SHOCKING SKULLS

The *Allosaurus* skull shows us how such massive monsters attacked their prey. Flexible joints in the *Allosaurus*'s jaw allowed it to gobble down huge chunks of meat. Flexibility was also a plus when the *Allosaurus* crashed with its mouth open into prey animals the size of small houses—the jaw joints acted as shock absorbers!

ROCKS FOR DINNER

Some plant-eating dinosaurs made up for their lack of chewing teeth by swallowing rocks, much as birds do today. The rocks, known as gastroliths, ground around in the dinosaur's stomach, chewing the plants for it.

BALANCING ACT

When they stretched their huge heads forward as they burst from the trees toward their prey, these top-heavy hunters would have toppled over without their heavy tails to balance them.

TERROR IN THE SKY

Pterosaurs (teh-ruh-SORES) were flying reptiles that lived at the same time as the dinosaurs. They dominated the skies before most birds. The wings of the pterosaur were made of a thin layer of elastic muscles covered with skin.

Rhamphorhynchus

From wing tip to wing tip, one *Quetzalcoatlus* (kwet-zal-COAT-lus) was as wide as a fighter jet!

PTRULY PTERRIBLE

The really big pterosaurs didn't appear until about 100 million years ago. *Pteranodon* (teh-RANN-uh-don) was a tailless monster with a big, bony crest at the back of its skull. Scientists speculate that the 6-foot-long crest might have helped the reptile steer and maintain stability as it flew. The largest pterosaur, *Quetzalcoatlus*, had a wingspan of up to 40 feet!

FIRST FLAMINGO?

One pterosaur managed to beat the flamingo to the art of shrimp fishing! Millions of years before flamingos existed, *Pterodaustro* (teh-roh-DAW-stroh) was equipped with a very bristly bottom jaw, which it would have used like a sieve to filter out small shrimplike animals from mouthfuls of water.

A BIT BATTY

Rhamphorhynchus (RAM-foh-RING-khus) was a late-Jurassic pterosaur that was about the size of a seagull and looked something like a big bat. It had a diamond-shaped rudder at the end of its tail and very long, sharp teeth that pointed forward—perfect for stabbing fish.

BRAIN BONUS

The feeding habits of which modern bird are similar to **Pteranodon**'s?
a) hummingbird
b) robin
c) pelican

What did pterosaurs have in common with modern birds?
a) long tail feathers
b) hollow bones
c) migration patterns

Which living bird has claws like a pterosaur's halfway along its wing?
a) hoatzin chick
b) Australian parrot
c) None of them, silly!

(answers on page 32)

FISH FINGER

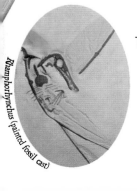

Rhamphorhynchus (painted fossil cast)

The pterosaur's wing bone was actually a very long fourth finger—the other three were short, probably used for grasping prey and climbing trees. Since some pterosaur fossils are found in prehistoric seabeds, scientists once thought that those creatures swam underwater. Now they think they were just dedicated fish-eaters!

MONSTERS OF THE DEEP

While dinosaurs ruled the land, other reptiles thrived at sea. They hunted many kinds of sea life, from fish, squid, and other reptiles to shellfish and various crunchy snacks from the seabed. Some were truly monstrous!

HERE BE MONSTERS!

The long-necked *Elasmosaurus* (ee-LAS-moh-SORE-us) would have been a scary sight—it was longer than a giant dump truck! Scientists think it was a stealthy fish-hunter: as it swam underwater, it may have stretched its long neck forward above the waves to snap up unsuspecting fish with a sudden overhead strike.

PLESIOSAURS TODAY?

Although a family of prehistoric sea reptiles called plesiosaurs (PLEE-see-oh-sores) died out at the same time as the dinosaurs, some people believe that the Loch Ness monster in Scotland is a living survivor. Unfortunately, there is no scientific evidence for this belief. Sea turtles are the only sea reptiles still living.

REPTILE RULES

Because they were reptiles, not fish, sea reptiles had to come to the surface to breathe air through their lungs. Most probably had to clamber onto a beach to lay eggs, just as modern-day sea turtles do. But they kept adapting to sea life. *Ichthyosaurus* may have learned to give birth to live young in the water, increasing the likelihood of their survival.

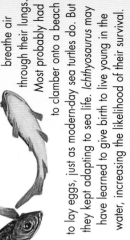

Elasmosaurus

TURTLEY AMAZING!

Archelon (ARK-eh-lon) was a giant sea turtle—more than 20 feet long. That's about four times bigger than the giant sea turtles alive today!

YE OLDE DOLPHINNE

Ichthyosaurus (IKH-thee-oh-SORE-us) was the first complete marine reptile fossil ever found. Two children, Mary Anning and her brother, Joseph, found the fossils by accident, in England in 1810. When the creature was alive, *Ichthyosaurus* looked like a very big, streamlined dolphin with a pointy beak.

BRAIN BONUS

The neck of *Elasmosaurus* was more than ____ its total length.

a) one quarter
b) one third
c) one half

What does the name *Ichthyosaurus* mean?

a) "fish reptile"
b) "dolphin cousin"
c) "spear nose"

What kind of insect has lived on Earth since long before the dinosaurs?

a) butterfly
b) cockroach
c) bee

(answers on page 32)

BRAIN BONUS

What is the long, narrow snout of the crocodile perfectly suited for?

a) digging
b) eating plants
c) catching fish

Why was Baron Georges Cuvier ahead of his time?

a) He was a time traveler.
b) He believed in the idea of extinction.
c) He owned a computer.

What is an ammonite?

a) a giant sea snail
b) a sort of shelled squid
c) a super-lobster

(answers on page 32)

WHALE MEAT AGAIN!

Mosasaurus was as big as today's biggest killer whales—and had much pointier teeth!

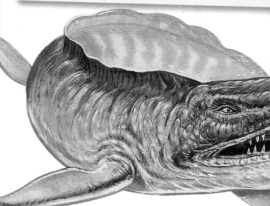

CAPTAIN CRUNCH

Mosasaurus cruised the seas, making a meal of anything it found. Its huge jaws could swing unusually wide to get its teeth into very meaty prey. But it ate shellfish, too—scientists have found several fossils of the heavily armored ammonite mollusk with mosasaur tooth holes crunched through their thick shells!

CROCOSAURUS

Some early crocodile ancestors ran across land on two legs, evolving over millions of years into the first dinosaurs. Other ancient crocodiles thrived in seas and rivers. When the dinosaurs died out, sea crocodiles also became extinct. But those that lived in rivers survived. Modern river crocs are considered to be the nearest living reptile relatives of dinosaurs.

KILLER CROCS & SUPER-LIZARDS

Of all the sea monsters in the dinosaur age, the most
horrible to meet looked very much like modern-day
crocodiles, only a lot bigger. Their bodies were streamlined
for speedy swimming and they spent their time hunting
other sea creatures—as well as each other!

FEARSOME FAMILY

Members of the mosasaur (MOH-zuh-sore) family were the
scariest lizards ever! They looked like huge crocodiles, but
they had flippers that made them very strong
swimmers. *Mosasaurus* itself, the big daddy
of the mosasaur family, grew to an
amazing 30 feet in length (as long as
a cement truck!), with jaws filled
with sharp teeth.

Mosasaurus

MONSTER MINE

The first *Mosasaurus* skull was
found by astonished Dutch chalk
miners in 1770, long before we
knew about dinosaurs. Fortunately for
science, the skull was stolen by Napoleon in 1795
and taken to Paris. Baron Georges Cuvier

Mosasaurus skull

(1769–1832) was a pioneering French scientist who knew a great
deal about animal anatomy. He studied the skull and correctly
concluded that it belonged to a giant lizard.

AWESOME ARMOR

In such a dangerous world, hefty plant-eaters had to develop a range of special defenses to avoid becoming someone else's lunch. Sometimes a few spikes were enough to scare their enemies away—but if those didn't work, having a skin that predators would break their teeth on was a big help!

FEARSOME FRILL

Triceratops didn't bother with full body armor. It had a bony frill at the back of its skull that extended over the neck, protecting its spine from a paralyzing *T-rex* bite. Mounted on its head were three huge horns. If a *T-rex* missed with its first bite, it could find itself impaled on those deadly horns— each one more than 3 feet long!

Triceratops

DIMWIT DINO

Although *Stegosaurus* could reach 25 feet long, its brain was only about the size of a walnut.

20

STING IN THE TAIL

Stegosaurus (STEG-oh-SORE-us) had a formidable defensive structure, including four big spikes in its tail for swiping at attackers. Its name means "roofed lizard." When scientists first found *Stegosaurus* skeletons, they thought the large bony plates lay flat over its back like protective roof tiles. More research showed that the plates probably stood upright and were not very useful for defense.

Stegosaurus

TANKYLOSAURUS

The most heavily armored animal ever to walk the Earth was *Ankylosaurus* (see pages 4–5). Weighing several tons, and measuring about 20 feet long, it grew special bony plates in the skin all along its back and sides. These fused together to form a shield like that of an armadillo.

NICE TO BEAT YOU

If you saw an ankylosaur wagging its tail, you wouldn't mistake this gesture for a friendly invitation! At the end of its tail, the bony plates in its skin grew into huge clubs, up to 3 feet across. Under attack, the ankylosaur would remain low to the ground, letting predators break their teeth on its skin and giving them a smack with its skull-shattering club tail.

BRAIN BONUS

How did *Ankylosaurus* protect its eyes from attack?

a) It used its tail as a shield.
b) It tucked its head in.
c) It had bony eyelids.

During what period did *Ankylosaurus* live?

a) Triassic (200 mya)
b) Jurassic (150 mya)
c) Cretaceous (70 mya)

What do we think the "roof tiles" of the *Stegosaurus* might have been used for?

a) defense
b) temperature control
c) digestion

(answers on page 32)

BRAIN BONUS

Which dinosaur had the biggest head?

a) *Corythosaurus*
b) *Torosaurus*
c) *Psittacosaurus*

What does *Triceratops* mean?

a) "three-horned face"
b) "rhinoceros cousin"
c) "the horned king"

What did some hadrosaurs use their broad, ducklike beaks for?

a) as a means of defense
b) snorkeling
c) scooping up leaves

(answers on page 32)

FULL SPEED AHEAD!

Triceratops used its three sharp horns to charge unlucky enemies.

BIRD BRAIN?

Psittacosaurus (si-tak-oh-SORE-us), or "parrot lizard," had a very strange skull. It had only a few teeth, but its sharp, hooked beak could slice through tough plants, just like a modern-day parrot's.

NOSY NEIGHBORS

Some hadrosaurs, such as *Corythosaurus* (koh-rith-oh-SORE-us), had very specialized hollow crests on their skulls. Fossils can't tell us what organs might have existed in these hollows, but scientists think that their surfaces might have contained extremely sensitive smell receptors. These might have made it possible for hadrosaurs to use scents for communication. The crests might also have been used like trumpets, allowing hadrosaurs to make loud hooting noises.

Corythosaurus

BONEHEADS

The crest-headed hadrosaurs (HAD-roh-sores) and the dome-headed pachycephalosaurs (PAK-ee-SEF-a-loh-sores) had some of the weirdest skulls in the world. Since there is nothing like them alive today, scientists can only guess what these curious domes and crests were meant to do.

HELMET HEADS

Pachycephalosaurs had bizarre dome-shaped heads, sometimes surrounded by a "crown" of blunt bumps. The dome was formed of 10 inches of solid bone, making the whole head into an extremely heavy battering ram. Males might have bashed each other with their heads to win mates, just as goats and sheep do today.

Pachycephalosaurs

DYNAMITE DEFENSE

NOSE PICK

The man who first assembled an *Iguanodon*'s skeleton was way off base. That's a *thumb* spike, not a horn!

Dinosaurs found some very inventive ways to defend themselves from attackers. If they didn't have thick, armorlike skin or bony heads to protect them, there were still some other tricks they could use.

HEADS OR TAILS?

Since actual dinosaur skin isn't preserved as a fossil, we will never know what colors and patterns dinosaurs had. But some scientists have speculated that ankylosaurs might have had eyespots on their club tails. Thinking that it was about to bite the ankylosaur's head, a *T-rex* would get a mouthful of club instead!

Iguanodon self-defense

THUMBS UP

The first dinosaur skeleton to be rebuilt, an *Iguanodon* (ig-WHA-no-don), was put together by fossil-hunter Gideon Mantell in 1835. A spike was found along with the skeleton, and Mantell decided that it belonged on the creature's nose! Scientists later discovered that the plant-eating *Iguanodon* had two thumb spikes that it used to stab would-be predators.

24

THE BIG WHIPPER

Giant sauropods, such as *Diplodocus* (di-PLOH-da-kus), had to have long tails to help balance their amazing necks. The thick part of the tail may have been useful for supporting the *Diplodocus* when it reached up into the trees, while the tail's stiff, bony end made a very effective whip to flick at predators.

CLEVER CAMO

Like deer and other modern-day plant-eaters, prehistoric herbivores were probably camouflaged in the shadows of forests and jungles. By holding very still, the patterns and colors of their skin would have blended into the background, making the defenseless animals invisible until the danger had passed.

Diplodocus

BRAIN BONUS

How big were footprints left by adult *Iguanodons*?

a) 36 inches long
b) 20 inches long
c) 12 inches long

What kind of land preserved the best dinosaur footprints?

a) desert
b) forest
c) swamp

Where are *Ankylosaurus* fossils not found?

a) Asia and America
b) Antarctica
c) Australia and India

(answers on page 32)

MOMMYSAURUS

Scientists used to think that dinosaurs buried their eggs and left their young to fend for themselves. But the *Maiasaura* (MY-ah-SORE-ah) earned its name "good mother lizard" after its nesting site was found in Montana in 1978. From clues around the nest, it was clear that this large dinosaur took great care of its young.

Maiasaura

BRAIN BONUS

What did most dinosaur eggshells feel like?

a) hard and bumpy
b) slimy
c) smooth

Dinosaur mothers laid their eggs...

a) in trees
b) in hollowed-out nests in the ground
c) on mounds of dirt

How long was a *Maiasaura* hatchling?

a 5 inches
b) 10 inches
c) 20 inches

(answers on page 32)

NICE NEST

Maiasaura may have nested in big colonies, as modern seabirds do. From trampled eggshells in the fossilized nests, we can tell that the young maiasaurs stayed in the nest for some time after hatching. The adults would have defended them from predators and perhaps brought them food.

VEGGYSAURUS

Most dinosaurs were plant-eaters, roaming the prehistoric landscape in harmless herds. *Iguanodon*, despite its size and its deadly thumb spikes, only had teeth for snipping plants and slicing them up.

NOT SO SCARY

Paleontologists can tell from fossils that some dinosaurs weren't at all scary. The teeth are the biggest clue: spiky, sharp teeth are usually for cutting meat; wide, flat teeth are more likely to be used for chewing plants.

Therizinosaurus

CLAWFULLY NICE?

Therizinosaurus (thair-a-ZINE-a-sore-us), or "scythe lizard," had claws that were over 2 feet long! Although scientists have found only parts of this beast's skeleton, many paleontologists think that it was not a dangerous predator. It had a small head and very small teeth—not very useful for tearing through chunks of meat. It might have used its monstrous claws to spear fish or scratch at termite mounds.

WHO ARE YOU CALLING CHICKEN?

Compsognathus (komp-soh-NAY-thus) was roughly chicken-sized! It could run very fast and lived on a diet of insects and frogs.

DINOSTARS

Everyone enjoys a good monster story, so dinosaurs are very popular with filmmakers...even though they have all been dead for about 65 million years.

Scene from Jurassic Park

CUSTOMIZED CROCODILES

Filmmakers can't hire dinosaurs as extras, so they have to use special effects. People in dinosaur costumes were often used in old movies. The alternative was to glue strange frills and bumps onto lizards and film them in slow motion.

Scene from The Last Dinosaur

BACK FROM THE DEAD

Before computer animation, some filmmakers used a technique called stop-motion photography. This involved making clay models and moving them by hand into slightly different positions for each frame of film. When the individual frames were all run together through the movie projector, the movement looked smooth and continuous. This technology was brand-new in 1925 when a filmmaker teamed up with the famous writer Sir Arthur Conan Doyle to make a motion picture version of Doyle's dinosaur novel, *The Lost World*. They told the film's first audience that the images were real footage of live dinosaurs. The effect was so spectacular that everyone believed them!

DEFROST DANGER

Discoveries of frozen woolly mammoths in the permafrost of Alaska and Siberia several years ago caused a lot of excitement, and a few films were based on the idea that other prehistoric animals, such as frozen dinosaurs, could be brought back to life. In *The Last Dinosaur* (1977), some unfortunate oil prospectors in Antarctica even defrosted a *T-rex*!

DINO DNA

The dinosaurs in two recent movies, *Jurassic Park* (1993) and *The Lost World: Jurassic Park* (1997), were rescued from extinction by genetic science—using DNA from dinosaur blood fossilized inside an ancient mosquito. Is this really possible? Scientists don't think so. To re-create an extinct creature, you would need a full set of DNA blueprints. Since DNA is very fragile, it breaks down over time.

BRAIN BONUS

Gertie, the first big-screen dinosaur, appeared in...

a) 1912
b) 1920
c) 1935

In the film *One of Our Dinosaurs Is Missing*, what was everyone looking for?

a) a baby dinosaur
b) microfilm hidden in a dinosaur fossil
c) the exit

What made the Japanese film legend, Godzilla, really angry?

a) cold noodles
b) nuclear explosions
c) pop music

(*answers on page 32*)

FAME AT LAST!

The dinosaur with the longest name, *Micropachycephalosaurus*, was also one of the smallest. It was only 20 inches long!

BRAIN BONUS

Where has a 65-million-year-old meteorite crater been discovered?
a) Yucatán, Gulf of Mexico
b) London, England
c) Crater Lake, Oregon

Which of these theories has been suggested to explain dinosaur extinction?
a) A nuclear bomb exploded.
b) Mice ate all the dinosaur eggs.
c) Cavemen poisoned the water.

Which of these is the most ancient?
a) the turtle
b) the dragonfly
c) the shark

(answers on page 32)

DEADLY DUST

If a meteorite 6 miles wide crashed into Earth, it might fill the atmosphere with dust, blocking out the sun and causing freak wintry weather all over the world. A huge volcanic eruption would have the same effect. Plants and animals of all sizes, even underwater, would be lucky to survive.

Meteorite colliding with Earth

DARK STAR

Perhaps the most unusual theory is that our sun has an unseen partner, nicknamed Nemesis, which passes through the comet belt around our solar system once every 26 million years. Every time it does, thousands of comets tumble out of orbit, bombarding our part of space. Scientists in Chicago have found evidence for mass extinctions every 26 million years.

THEY'RE OUT THERE SOMEWHERE!

Modern birds are probably very close relatives to the last of the dinosaurs.

MORE DANGEROUS THAN DINOS

The extinction of dinosaurs and other creatures 65 million years ago is unexplained. There are all kinds of different theories, but all we really know is that something resulted in the death of all dinosaurs.

NOT DEAD, JUST DIFFERENT!

Not everyone agrees that dinosaurs died out suddenly. Some think that they evolved to meet new environmental conditions, perhaps becoming the first birds. *Archaeopteryx* (ark-ee-OP-ter-iks) first appeared around 140 million years ago, with clear signs (fossil impressions) of fully developed feathers. Was it a feathered dinosaur or a dinosaur-like bird? Both possibilities are correct, based on current research.

SUPER-SURVIVORS

Why did so many creatures die at the same time as the dinosaurs while others were unharmed? No one knows—but fossilized remains tell us that while giant meat-eaters and flying reptiles all died at the same time, birds survived, along with river crocodiles, crabs, lobsters, turtles, and insects such as the cockroach.

Archaeopteryx

BRAIN BONUS ANSWERS

p. 3 c) a fossil. Any naturally occurring evidence of past life is also called a fossil—not just fossilized bones. a) b) c) In China, the fossils were thought to belong to ancient dragons, and the teeth were ground up and used in medicines. In Europe, some people believed the remains were the bones of giants or terrifying sea monsters. a) a footprint. This is called a trace fossil because it was never actually a part of a dinosaur.

p. 4 c) New Mexico. b) just past its knee. a) to pick their teeth. Sauropods probably balanced with their tails when they reared up to eat from treetops. They could also deliver a stinging blow with the ends of their tails, made up of slim, bony rods.

p. 7 a) at the very end. *T-rex* remains are found in rocks from the end of the Cretaceous Period, from 65 to 70 million years ago. b) teeth. Like many living animals, *T-rex* grew new teeth when the old, worn teeth fell out. That means there are lots more teeth to find than there are full skeletons. c) 7 feet.

p. 8 c) by the shape of their teeth. b) dig. Based on the shape and size of fossilized claws, paleontologists can make educated guesses as to what specialized purpose they might have had. a) There are no fossils found on the moon, but they are found on every continent on Earth.

p. 11 b) omnivores. c) ten times their size. b) from 300 to 600. They did not all live at the same time, and no one kind of dinosaur existed for the entire dinosaur age.

p. 12 b) Jurassic (150 mya). b) for a better grip on prey. a) In 1824, William Buckland of England described the *Megalosaurus*.

p. 15 c) pelican. b) hollow bones—to reduce their weight. a) hoatzin chick. The young of the hoatzin, a tropical South American bird, has claws in two places along each wing. As the chicks grow into adulthood, the claws disappear!

p. 17 c) one half. Its neck contained 28 vertebrae. A modern giraffe's neck has only seven! a) "fish reptile." b) cockroach.

p. 18 c) catching fish. b) He believed in the idea of extinction. b) a sort of shelled squid.

p. 21 c) It had bony eyelids. c) Cretaceous (70 mya). b) temperature control. Scientists speculate that *Stegosaurus* might have used the bony plates on its back to warm up (by exposing them to sunlight) or to cool down (by standing in the shade or in a cool breeze).

p. 22 b) *Torosaurus*. Its skull grew to 8 feet long—that's as long as a compact car! a) "three-horned face." c) scooping up leaves. Unlike the sauropods, who gulped down their food whole, hadrosaurs had special teeth to chew leaves and tough plants before they swallowed.

p. 25 a) 36 inches long. The *Iguanodon* could walk on two or four feet and was 30 feet long. c) swamp. Dinosaur tracks are most often found on land that was once soft and wet. Footprints were preserved when they filled with sand and mud. As the water dried up over time, this material fossilized, keeping a perfect impression of the tracks. c) Australia and India.

p. 26 a) hard and bumpy. b) in hollowed-out nests in the ground. c) 20 inches.

p. 29 a) 1912, in a movie of the same name. b) microfilm hidden in a dinosaur fossil. b) nuclear explosions.

p. 30 a) Yucatán, Gulf of Mexico. b) Mice ate all the dinosaur eggs. Many other theories have also been suggested. c) the shark.